Between the Lions
GET WILD ABOUT READING

# The Fox and the Crow

## Activity Storybook

**By Susan Ring**

**Based on the script by Norman Sti...**

**Illustrated by June Valentine-Rupp...**

D1224070

**A GOLDEN BOOK • NEW YORK**

Golden Books Publishing Company, Inc., New York, New York 10106

BETWEEN THE LIONS is a co-production of WGBH Boston and Sirius Thinking, Ltd. BETWEEN THE LIONS is funded in part by a grant from the United States Department of Education through the Corporation for Public Broadcasting. Major support is also provided by the Carnegie Corporation of New York, the Park Foundation, The Arthur Vining Davis Foundations, the Charles H. Revson Foundation, and the Institute for Civil Society. National corporate sponsorship is provided by Cheerios® and eToys®.

Theo was taking a quiet catnap in the library, when suddenly Lionel crept in. "She's here, Dad," Lionel said nervously, looking over his shoulder.

"Who's here?" asked Theo, waking up and wiping the sleep from his eyes.

"Leona," Lionel said. "She's here someplace, sneaking up on me and getting ready to—"

*Pounce!* In that instant, Leona appeared out of nowhere and jumped onto Lionel's back. "Gotcha again, Lionel!" she said, laughing.

Just then, Cleo walked in carrying a book. "Look at this beauty," she said. "It's a brand-new version of *The Fox and the Crow*, a fable by Aesop."

"Yum! Let's read it," said Theo eagerly.

"Wait for us!" shouted Walter and Clay Pigeon, hurrying down from their perch in the dome of the library. Walter and Clay never missed a chance to hear a story about birds.

Everyone gathered around Theo as he began the story. . . .

One day a fox took a walk in the woods. The fox saw a crow in a tree. The crow had a tiny but tasty-smelling piece of cheese in her beak. "Mmmmm! That is one tiny but tasty-smelling piece of cheese!" said the fox.

"Hey, that reminds me," said Lionel. "What kind of cheese can you live in?"

"I don't know," said Leona. "What kind?"

"Cottage cheese!" Lionel said. Everyone laughed at Lionel's joke.

The fox wanted that cheese. She had to think of a way to get the crow to drop it.

"The crow won't drop the cheese," said Walter. "That bird is too . . . too . . ."

"Smart?" asked Clay.

"Yeah, smart," said Walter. "But still, I can't look."

"Me neither," said Clay. Both pigeons covered their eyes. But then they peeked out from between their wings to see what would happen next.

The fox looked up at the crow. "Look at that beautiful bird!" she said. "If that bird could sing, then she would be queen of all birds."

The Fox and the Crow by Aesop

"What do you think that crow will do, Daddy?" Leona asked. "Let him read and we'll find out," said Lionel impatiently. "Okay," said Leona. "Read on, Daddy."

The crow wanted to be known as the queen of all birds, so she opened her beak and let out a "caw!" Unfortunately, she also let out the tiny piece of cheese.

The crow watched the small piece of cheese drop, drop, and drop. It did not stop until it popped in the fox's mouth with a tiny *kerplop*.

The Fox and the Crow
by Aesop

"The cheese goes *kerplop*!" said Leona, laughing as she gave Lionel a playful bop on his head.

"Cut it out, Leona," said Lionel. "The cheese went *kerplop* in the fox's mouth—not on her head!"

The fox swallowed the cheese and said, "That was deliciously cheesy and surprisingly easy." And she ran off into the woods with a skip and a hop.

"The crow learned a very big lesson," Theo continued.

"If you want to hang on to your cheese, don't sing?" asked the crow from inside the book.

"No," said Theo. "Beware of flatterers. They are people who say nice things about you just to get something from you."

"The end," said Theo, closing the book.

"Boo! Boo! Bad!" cried Walter and Clay in an uproar.

"I take it you birds find the story offensive?" asked Theo.

"Yes! It makes birds look like birdbrains!" said Clay.

"We don't like books that make birds look like birdbrains!" added Walter.

Cleo had an idea. "Why don't you rewrite the story?" she suggested. "You could have the crow be the hero this time."

Walter and Clay liked this idea, and so did Lionel and Leona. They all rushed off to begin writing the new version of *The Fox and the Crow*—a story in which birds would rule.

# The Fox and the Crow Has Got to Go!

Walter and Clay think *The Fox and the Crow* makes birds look like birdbrains! See how many 3-letter words you can make from the letters in this sentence:

# Birds are not birdbrains!

# Where Are the Words?

Lionel and Leona are helping Walter and Clay write *The New Fox and the Crow*. But extra letters appear each time they type a word on their computer. Can you help them? Circle the real word on each line of letters below.

1. b f o x k l
2. t c r o w b j
3. q s d r o p k j
4. y c h e e s e l b
5. r v e r y c v

# Look for the Books

As Lionel and Leona write their story, Theo and Cleo hunt for some books of their own. They're looking for books with a word in the title that rhymes with **fox**. See how many you can find. Then circle the books.

# Secret Message

"Look," says Scot.
"Chicken Jane is trying to tell
us something."

"I do not know what
Chicken Jane is saying," says Dot.

Solve the secret message to find out what Chicken Jane
is trying to tell Scot and Dot. Each letter stands for the letter that
comes before it in the alphabet. (For example, n = m)

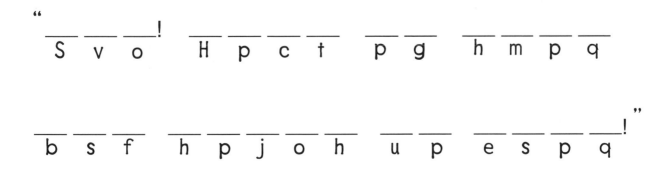

"__ __ __ ! __ __ __ __ __ __ __ __ __ __
  S v o   H p c t   p g   h m p q

__ __ __ __ __ __ __ __ __ __ __ __ __ __ __ !"
b s f   h p j o h   u p   e s p q

# In the Beginning

Just like stories, words also have a beginning, a middle, and an end. Draw a line connecting each picture below with the letter it begins with.

b

c

t

l

f

# Word Power

All the words below want to change. Dr. Wordheimer can make this happen—with your help. Change one letter in each word below so that it becomes a *new* word that describes the picture next to it.

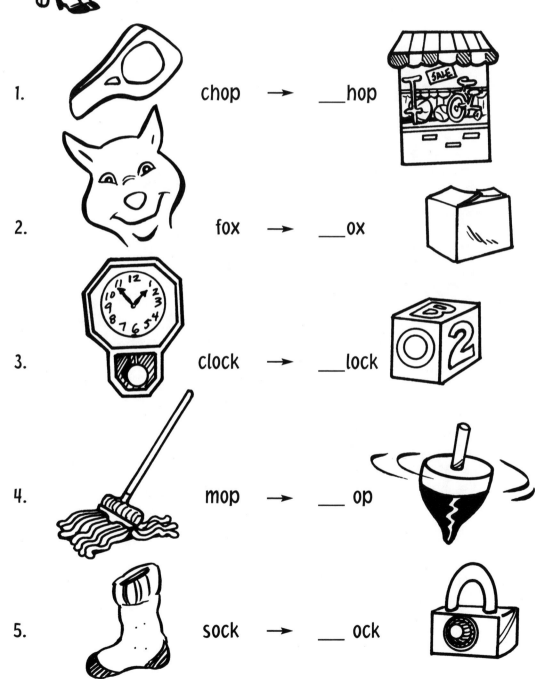

1.   chop   →   ___hop

2.   fox   →   ___ox

3.   clock   →   ___lock

4.   mop   →   ___op

5.   sock   →   ___ock

# The Great Smartini

The Great Smartini has done it again! He put 3 words into his magic smarty-pants and then pulled out the animals shown here. Which 3 words did The Great Smartini put into his magic smarty-pants? Circle them. Then put them in the correct order on the lines below.

**sloppy     ox     frogs     boxing     hopping     spotted     mop**

_____     _____     _____

What vowel letter appears in all of these words? _____

# Gawain's Word!

Sir **p** and Sir **op** have charged together to make the word **pop**.

Besides Sir **p,** what other knights do you know that could charge together with Sir **op** to make new words? Write the correct letter or letters in each of the flags below.

ch  t  h  c  m

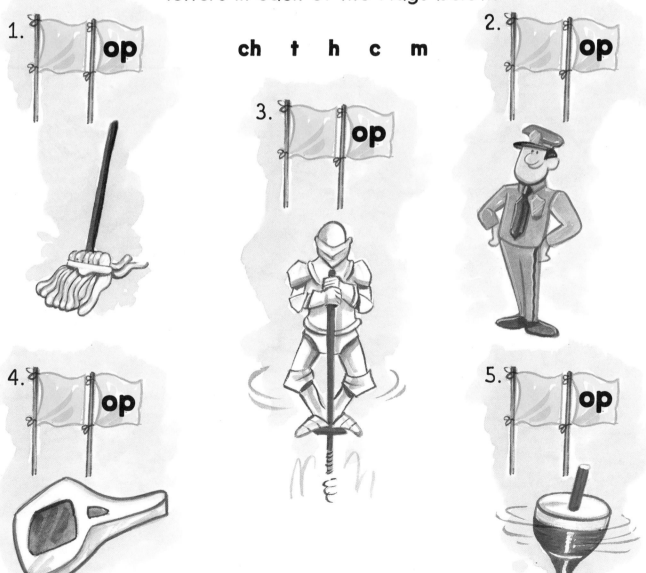

1. op

2. op

3. op

4. op

5. op

# Birds Rule! Birds Are Cool!

Follow the directions below to find a secret picture of one of Walter and Clay's feathered friends. When you're done, unscramble the underlined letters to spell out the name of the bird in the spaces below.

Color the spaces with words that rhyme with **hop** brow<u>n</u>.
Color the spaces with words that rhyme with **sock** <u>r</u>ed.
Color the spaces with words that rhyme with **dot** p<u>i</u>nk.
Color the spaces with words that rhyme with **log** <u>b</u>lack.
Color the spaces with words that rhyme with **rob** yell<u>o</u>w.

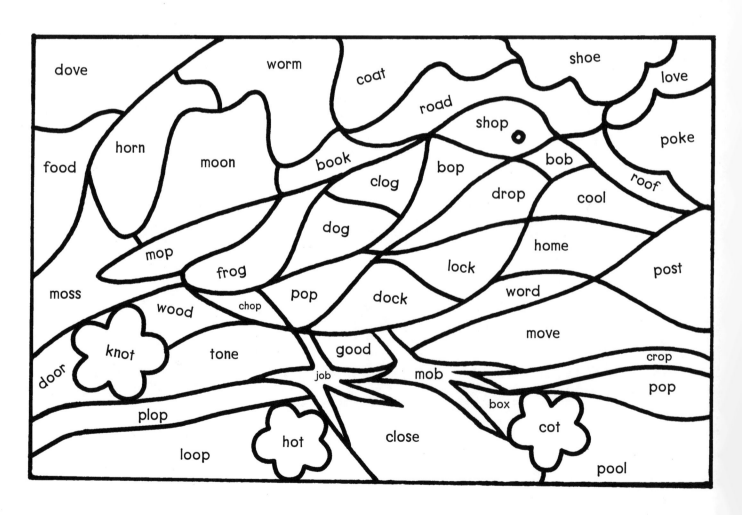

# What's the Combination?

Leona loves to learn new words! Can you help her spell the words pictured below? First, draw lines connecting the letters in List A to the letters in List B. Then write the correct word below each picture. We've done one for you.

1. __log__

2. _____

3. _____

| List A | List B |
|--------|--------|
| b | ock |
| cl | op |
| m | og |
| kn | ot |
| l | ob |
| p | ox |

4. _____

5. _____

6. _____

**BONUS:** How many more words can you make by combining letters from List A with the letters in List B? _____

_____

19

# What's Cooking with Theo and Cleo?

Theo and Cleo are making Hot Chop Cheese Drop Soup in a Pot with No Top. Can you circle all the things they need for this recipe?

## Hot Chop Cheese Drop Soup in a Pot with No Top

1. Find a **pot with no top**.
2. Drop one big piece of **cheese** in the pot with no top.
3. Drop **chop** in the pot with no top.
4. Look at the **clock**. Cook for 3 hours in the pot with no top.

# Chop-Chop-Chop

Just like the **chop** in Theo and Cleo's recipe, the answers to the clues below all have **op** in them. Using the pictures to help you, can you figure out the words?

1. The opposite of bottom      ___ op

2. A policeman      ___ op

3. What you use to clean the floor      ___ op

4. Let fall to the ground      ___ ___ op

5. Another word for a store      ___ ___ op

21

# Soggy Bottom

Lionel wrote a silly poem about a fox. Can you finish it using these words?

**socks**      **rocks**      **slop**      **kerplop**      **hot**      **spot**

### Soggy Bottom

by Lionel the Lion

A fox was feeling _____,

So she went to a cooler _____.

She put on a pair of _____

To walk on some slippery _____.

But the rocks were full of _____,

So the fox fell down and went _____!

# The Odd One Out

Leona wants to write a poem, too. You can help her. Here is a list of rhyming words. But in each group of words, one word doesn't rhyme. Figure out which one doesn't belong and cross it out.

1. chop     cop     goat

2. cat     pot     knot

3. log     foot     frog

4. brick     lock     block

Now write your own poem using some of the rhyming words above. Make it as silly as you like.

_____

_____

_____

_____

# Drop, Drop, *Kerplop!*

In *The Fox and the Crow*, the tiny piece of cheese went drop, drop, *kerplop*—right into the fox's mouth! Lead the piece of cheese from the crow to the fox. When you're finished, write each letter you passed in order on the lines below to find out what the fox would love to have with her cheese.

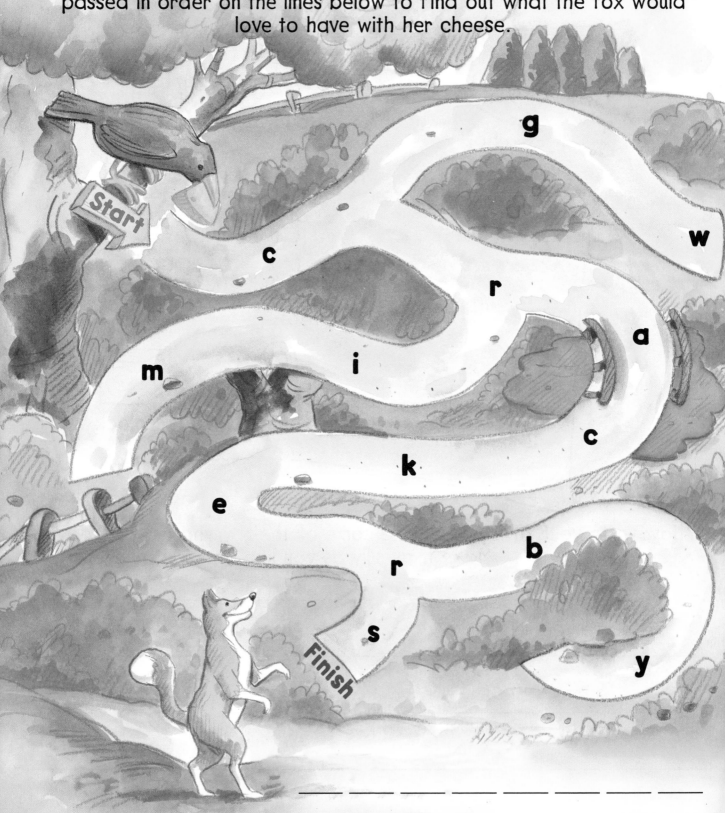

\_\_\_\_ \_\_\_\_ \_\_\_\_ \_\_\_\_ \_\_\_\_ \_\_\_\_ \_\_\_\_ \_\_\_\_

# Tiger Words

Help Tiger Words step up to the **t** and finish the words below. Using the pictures as clues, write the correct missing letters on the blank spaces below.

1. __ __ t

2. __ __ __ t

3. __ __ __ t

4. __ __ t

5. __ __ t

# Aesop's Fable

Click the Mouse is helping Walter and Clay Pigeon write a letter to Aesop, the author of *The Fox and the Crow*. Choose the word from the list below that fits best into each blank.

**not      hero      fool      crow**

**story      fox      Aesop**

Dear _____,

    We do _____ like your story. It makes the

_____ look like a birdbrain! The _____ was

not nice to _____ the crow. Next time, please

make the crow the _____. We think that would

be a better _____. Thank you.

                                        Sincerely,
                                        Walter and Clay

# What's in a Name?

Heath knows lots of words. See how many words of
3 letters or more you can make from the letters in his name:

# Heath the Thesaurus

_____    _____    _____

_____    _____    _____

_____    _____    _____

_____    _____    _____

_____    _____    _____

# Tongue Twister Time

Try saying this tongue twister five times fast:
**Scot's sloppy spotted socks got soggy.**

Now make up your own tongue twisters using some of these words:

| | | | |
|---|---|---|---|
| blobs | frogs | hot | plop |
| floppy | globs | of | slop |
| foggy | hogs | on | top |

_____

_____

_____

_____

_____

# The Great Smartini

The Great Smartini has done it again! He put 4 words into his magic smarty-pants and then pulled out the animals shown here. Which 4 words did The Great Smartini put into his magic smarty-pants? Circle them. Then put them in the correct order on the lines below.

**on      not      sloppy      plop      logs      jot      poppy      hogs**

_____  _____  _____  _____

What vowel letter appears in all of these words? _____

# A Very Big Puzzle

For the ending to their new story, Leona thinks the crow should have a very, very, very, very, very, very, very, very big piece of cheese. Heath the Thesaurus knows lots of words that mean **very big**. Can you find them in the puzzle below? Look up, down, across, backward, and diagonally.

**huge**　　　　**large**　　　　**massive**
**gigantic**　　**giant**　　　　**jumbo**
**super**　　　　**great**　　　　**immense**

```
c  i  t  n  a  g  i  g
h  m  a  s  s  i  v  e
e  m  o  b  m  u  j  t
g  e  u  m  o  e  n  n
r  n  g  o  g  u  s  a
a  s  s  u  p  e  r  i
l  e  h  t  a  e  r  g
```

Now write all the leftover letters in order below
to spell one of the biggest big words of all!

___ ___ ___ ___ ___ ___ ___ ___ ___ ___

# Riddle Me This

Help Leona solve Lionel's riddle. Fill in the blanks with the correct missing letters to answer the clues below.

1. Work                            j ___ ___
                                         6

2. A snack at the movies    P ___ ___ c ___ ___ n
                                              2

3. A necklace with a picture   l ___ ___ k ___ ___
                                            9   5

4. To cut down a tree        ___ h ___ ___
                                      3

5. Messy                     ___ l ___ P ___ y
                             4

6. Cloudy                    ___ o ___ g ___
                             1

7. The sound a clock makes   t ___ c ___ ___ o ___ k
                                  7       8

Now write the numbered letters below to find out the answer to Lionel's riddle:

## What do you get when you cross a lion with a snowman?

___ ___ ___ ___ ___ ___ ___ ___ ___
 1   2   3   4   5   6   7   8   9

# Gawain's Word!

Sir **sp** and Sir **ot** have charged together to make the word **spot**.

Besides Sir **sp,** what other knights do you know that could charge together with Sir **ot** to make new words? Write the correct letter or letters in each of the flags below.

h    kn    p    D

1.  ot

2. 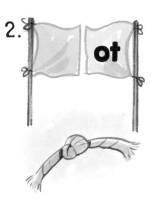 ot

3.  ot

4.  ot

# Make a Match

Lionel is reading a book about different jobs people do.
Draw a line from each job to its matching picture.

helicopter pilot

rock singer

clock maker

doctor

# Knock Knock

"You know what I think should happen
to the fox?" says Lionel.
"What?" asks Leona.
"Knock knock."
"Who's there?"
"Locket."
"Locket who?"
"Locket up and
throw away the key!"

Just like the words **knock** and **locket,** the
answers to these clues have **ock** in them.
Can you solve them all?

1. A key opens this    ___ ock

2. Wooden toys    ___ ___ ock ___

3. A spaceship    ___ ock ___ ___

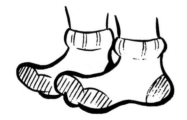

4. You wear these on your feet    ___ ock ___

5. It tells time    ___ ___ ock

# A Cheesy Story

Sam Spud has written his own version of *The Fox and the Crow*. But he made some spelling mistakes that changed the meaning of the story. Read the silly story. Then fix the misspelled words and read the story again.

The name is Spud, Sam Spud. There was a **knack** at the door.
_____

A crow **hipped** into the room. He wanted me to **drip** everything
_____                                          _____

and find the **fax** who **rubbed** him of his cheese. I told him
_____        _____

I did not want the **jab** because it was cheesy. The crow said
_____

he would **ship** around. He let out a "**cow!**" and flew out
_____                              _____

of the room.

## And now, back to our story!

Everyone gathered together in the library to hear the new version of the story.

"I'd like to present *The New Fox and the Crow*," said Lionel, "written by Lionel the Lion!"

"And Leona the Lion," Leona quickly added.

"And Click the Mouse, who scanned the pictures and printed the book!" said Click, beaming with pride.

"It's dedicated to birds everywhere!" said Walter Pigeon.

"Because birds rule!" exclaimed Clay Pigeon.

"Birds are cool!" added Walter Pigeon.

"Can we get on with it?" Lionel asked impatiently. He then began to read. . . .

A fox was walking in the woods one day. The fox saw a crow in a tree. The crow had a very, very, very, very, very, very big piece of cheese in her beak.

"Don't you like the 'very, very, very big' part?" asked Leona.
"Yes, very, very, very much," said Cleo.
"That was my idea," said Leona. "Lionel wanted to say 'humongous.'"
"Humongous is a good word, too," said Theo.

"Look at that beautiful bird," the fox said. "If she could sing, she would be queen of all birds."

The New Fox and the Crow

"Hey! This doesn't sound very different so far," said Walter.
"Yeah! This is almost the same story," said Clay, ruffling her feathers.
"Except for the 'very' part," Leona reminded them.
"Just keep listening," said Lionel, and he continued to read.

The crow opened her beak and let out a "caw!" She also let out the very, very, very, very, very, very big piece of cheese.

"Oh, no! The fox is tricking her again," cried Clay. "I can't look!" She hid her head behind her wings.

"Maybe you guys weren't listening," said Walter, "but you were supposed to make the bird *not* look like a . . ."

"Birdbrain," said Clay.

"Just wait," said Leona. "You'll love the ending. I promise!"

The crow watched the cheese drop, drop, and drop onto the fox's head with a very, very, very, very, very, very big *kerplop!*

The New

Walter and Clay fluttered their wings with delight. "The cheese landed on the fox's head, instead of in her mouth!" said Clay, laughing.

"I love it!" said Walter.

"But the cheese still went *kerplop*!" said Leona, and she plopped her paw on Lionel's head again.

"Stop that, Leona!" said Lionel. "I'm trying to read."

"Ouch!" cried the fox.
The crow laughed. "Haw! Haw!"

"And the fox learned a very big lesson," continued Lionel.
"Sometimes flatterers get flattened?" asked the fox from inside the book.
"No. Not all birds are birdbrains!" said Lionel.

"The end," said Lionel.

"Bravo!" said Theo, clapping his hands. Everyone loved *The New Fox and the Crow*, especially Walter and Clay.

"Hooray for the crow!" cried Clay.

"She's a hero for birds everywhere!" said Walter, puffing up with pride.

And so, with hard work and a little imagination, Lionel, Leona, and Click created a new ending everyone could enjoy. But it did not impress Busterfield, who had been listening all along.

"Very clever, but it's not as good as the original," he said. "No one will want to read it."

Just then, a chicken entered the library. "Bawk!" she clucked. "I'd like to read *The New Fox and the Crow*."

"Hmph!" exclaimed Busterfield. "Chickens don't count."

# What's the Difference?

When you use your imagination, anything can happen in a story! In the lines below, write what happened in the first story (pages 4–9). Then write what changed in the second story (pages 37–42). Finally, use your imagination to think of how else the story might change.

1. a. In the first story: The piece of cheese was _____.

   b. In the second story: The piece of cheese was _____

   _____.

   c. Use your imagination! The piece of cheese could be _____

   _____.

2. a. In the first story: The piece of cheese fell in the fox's _____.

   b. In the second story: The piece of cheese fell on the fox's _____.

   c. Use your imagination! The piece of cheese could fall _____

   _____.

3. a. In the first story: The _____ learned a very big lesson.

   b. In the second story: The _____ learned a very big lesson.

   c. Use your imagination! _____ could learn a very big lesson.

# Go for It!

Now it's your turn to rewrite *The Fox and the Crow*! First, follow the directions below to make your own book. Then, using your ideas, write your own version of the story. Don't forget to draw pictures to go with it.

## Here's what you do:

1. Carefully cut out the next page.

2. With the black-and-white side facing you, fold the page across on the solid line. Then fold the page down.

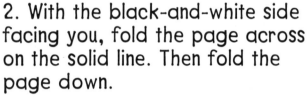

3. Staple the book together on the dashed lines on the cover page.

4. Carefully cut the pages at the top of the book as shown.

5. Write your story on the pages with blank lines. Draw a picture to go with each page. Make sure you draw a picture on the cover, too!

The New Fox and the Crow

by
_____

This book was
created by

_____
(write your name)

on _____ _____ 20_____
(month)        (day)      (year)

_____
_____
_____
_____
_____
_____
_____
_____
_____

_____

_____

_____

_____

_____

_____

_____

_____

_____

_____

_____

_____

_____

_____

_____

_____

_____

# ANSWERS

## page 10
Some possible answers:
aid, and, ant, bad, bar, bat, bib, bid, bit, bob, dab, den, did, dot, eat, net, oat, ode, ore, ram, rat, rib, rid, rob, rod, rot, sad, sat, sir, sit, tan, tin

## page 11
1. fox
2. crow
3. drop
4. cheese
5. very

## page 12
*How to Fix a Jack-in-the-Box*

*How to Cure Your Chicken Pox*

*How to Raise a Pet Ox*

## page 13
Run! Gobs of glop are going to drop!

## page 14

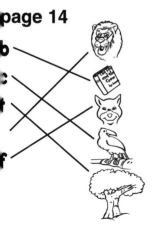

## page 15
1. shop
2. box
3. block
4. top
5. lock

## page 16
hopping spotted frogs *or* spotted hopping frogs
The letter **o** appears in all of these words.

## page 17
1. mop
2. cop
3. hop
4. chop
5. top

## page 18

**robin**

## page 19
1. log
2. pot
3. knob
4. clock
5. mop
6. box
Some possible answers for BONUS: bop, bog, clog, mop, knot, lot, pop

## page 20

## page 21
1. top
2. cop
3. mop
4. drop
5. shop

## page 22
A fox was feeling _hot_,
So she went to a cooler _spot_.
She put on a pair of _socks_
To walk on some slippery _rocks_.
But the rocks were full of _slop_,
So the fox fell down and went _kerplop!_

## page 23
1. goat
2. cat
3. foot
4. brick

## page 24

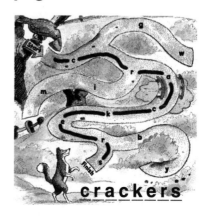

c r a c k e r s

## page 25
1. pot
2. knot
3. Scot
4. hot
5. Dot

## page 26

Dear ___Aesop___ ,

We do ___not___ like your story. It makes the ___crow___ look like a birdbrain! The ___fox___ was not nice to ___fool___ the crow. Next time, please make the crow the ___hero___. We think that would be a better ___story___. Thank you.

Sincerely,
Walter and Clay

## page 27
Some possible answers:
are, art, ate, ear, east, eat, hat, hear, heat, hut, rat, rate, rest, rust, ruts, sat, sea, seat, see, set, share, she, sheet, tar, tart, tea, teeth, test, that, the, there, these

## page 29
sloppy hogs on logs
The vowel letter **o** appears in all of these words.

## page 30

```
c (i  t  n  a  g  i  g)
h (m  a  s  s  i  v  e)
e  m (o  b  m  u  j) t
g  e  u  m  o (e) n  n
r  n  n  g  o  g  u  s  a
a  s (s  u  p  e  r) i
l  e (h  t  a  e  r  g)
```

**humongous**

## page 31
1. job
2. popcorn
3. locket
4. chop
5. sloppy
6. foggy
7. ticktock
**frostbite**

## page 32
1. pot
2. knot
3. Dot
4. hot

## page 33
helicopter pilot

rock singer

clock maker

doctor

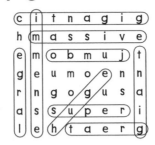

## page 34
1. lock
2. blocks
3. rocket
4. socks
5. clock

## page 35
knack = knock
hipped = hopped
drip = drop
fax = fox
rubbed = robbed
jab = job
ship = shop
cow = caw

## page 43
1. a. tiny
   b. very, very, very, very, very, very big

2. a. mouth
   b. head

3. a. crow
   b. fox